SEWING A FRIENDSHIP

Written and Illustrated by

Natalie Tinti

TintiNatie

If you shall have any comments or questions
about other Natalie's works please feel free
to contact the author at o.tinti@hotmail.com
or visit our web site at www tintinatie.com

In dedication to my parents,

Crystal, Peter, Grandma,

Luda, my teachers, and my

friends for inspiring and

helping me write this book.

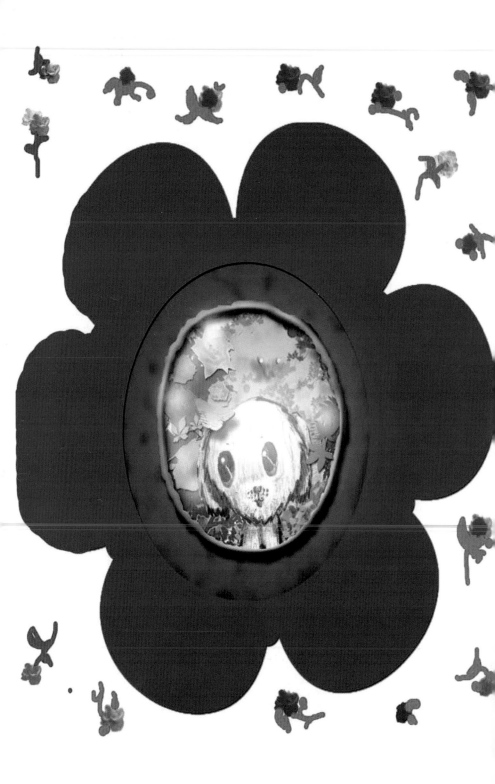

Foreword....

It is truly a privilege to introduce Natalie Tinti, a 10 year old creative genius in her own right. The idea for this book came about quite surprisingly one afternoon when my 8 year old daughter Emily and Natalie were playing. It was summertime and Natalie was showing me some pictures she had drawn and some stories she had written for school. As you will see, the pictures took my breath away. Each picture told a story, each character had a personality which was colorful, creative and unique. In that moment, Natalie saw that her own expression through stories and art could go way beyond school and so she began to create this book. Having written 5 books of my own, I am inspired by how easily and effortlessly her ideas came to life. She has discovered her voice at such a young age and is now committed to making that available for other young writers. You will touch by her heart, moved by her stories, and inspired by her values.

By: Crystal Neels

Table of Contents

INTRODUCTION
of CHARACTERS

Sokron Blossom

Birthday: January 5

Age: 7

Family:

Brothers

Peter, Thomas, David, Jonny

Sister Emily

Mom, Dad and Grandma

Eye color: Blue

Hair color: Blonde

Favorite food: Chocolate strawberries

Favorite color: Pink

Specialty: Visual artist

Nina Key

Birthday: December 15

Age: 7

Family: Sister Mindy

       Dad

Eye color: Blue

Hair color: Blonde

Favorite food: Chocolate cookie dough

Favorite color: Violet

Specialty: Sensitive to sound and music

13

Meeka Venya

Birthday: May 5

Age: 7

Family:

Mom

Eye color: Blue

Hair color: Orange

Favorite food: Ice cream

Favorite color: Red

Specialty: Loves numbers and math

problems

Jonsy Jipsy

Birthday: March 10

Age: 7

Family: Mom and Dad

Eye color: Brown

Hair color: Brown

Favorite food: Salmon

Favorite color: Yellow

Specialty: Sensitive to feelings

Kiki Shaver

Birthday: November 19

Age: 9

Family:

Uncle Vincent and Aunt Scarlett

Eye color: Brown

Hair color: Black

Favorite food: Bread

Favorite color: Black

Specialty: Sensitive to feelings

19

Babushka
(Grandma)

Birthday: March 4

Age: 67

Family: Sokron's

Eye color: Gray

Hair color: Gray

Favorite food: Figs

Favorite color: White

Specialty: Helps improves friendships
and the master of Dogon

21

Dogon

Birthday: June 8   Age: 18

Hair color: Brown

Favorite food: Cat Food

Favorite color: White

Specialty: Secret agent Eyes color:
Blue & Purple

Chapter 1

JOURNEY of the WIND

The beautiful, twinkling, shining stars pulled away all wishes that were made that night by everyone, everyone, everyone. A mysterious moon twirled to other places, letting the sun have a chance to shine. The sun finished its duties on the other side of the world and rose from the hills turning into a bright sunrise and let all light come out to share its love and happiness with everything that day. All the trees smiled happier than ever for they saw the light in their faces. The flowers opened up and bloomed, the birds woke up and chirped a morning song, and the wind twirled wonderful music around in colorful circles.

"Hey, look at this! Meeka Veniya is all ready for school!" the wind whispered as it traveled through the neighborhood.

Meeka always kept her long orange hair in her favorite two ponytails tied around with measuring tapes. Meeka loves school so much, that she would want to live there forever and ever. Sometimes she

24

would forget to take her school uniform off at night and use a text book as a pillow. Every evening Meeka would happily wait until the next school day so that she could do her brain developing exercises.

Meeka, an avid science student, looked outside and said, "I wonder how much H_2O will be in the air today."

In a nearby tree Meeka imagined a reply from the mocking birds, "Nine times nine is eighty-one, that is our reading for today", chirping in a language only a math person could understand.

"Thanks," Meeka replied.

Then she heard her mom's voice coming from the kitchen, "M-E-E-K-A, have you finished your lunch from yesterday?"

"No, M-O-M. I am going to finish it today. I'll be outside counting the clouds," Meeka answered, describing her favorite way to pass time before school.

As the wind blew further to the next house, it whooshed by and thought, "There is no way that any child will be awake in this house. It's only seven o'clock! Jonsy Jipsy is either dance sleeping or doing her morning exercises and fell asleep."

Jonsy Jipsy, a princess of her home kingdom, adores her beautiful brown hair. She loves to sing loudly songs that she would create while belly dancing in her yellow room. Her favorite subject at school would be PE and hanging upside down on the bars. That's why she does not like to wear dresses at any time.

Jonsy woke up from the floor that she fell onto while dancing in her sleep and ran to the window to look outside. Jonsy, the one who feels deeply about everything, felt that the day would be perfect, just like her.

"Darling, what do you feel like eating this morning?" her dad asked as he bowed.

"I feel like a cherry with vanilla ice cream, a cup of dragon tea with a yellow umbrella, and a huge hot chocolate cake," Jonsy sang joyfully.

"Yes my dear," he obediently replied.

The wind hurried forward to a brown house next door, and wondered out loud about the young girl who lived there, "Kiki Shaver, why a long face?"

This girl always would wear dark-colored clothes and believed that everyone around her was always disappointed with her.

Kiki lived with her aunt and uncle in a tiny house that she does not like at all.

"I don't even have my own room. It's so noisy in this living room where I have to sleep every night on that old broken gray coach, that I can't fall asleep until one o'clock in the morning," complained Kiki to herself.

"The only thing that I enjoy doing is reading my scary books in THAT back yard," Kiki complained as she described how she disliked the yard of her home.

Kiki looked through the kitchen window with a sad expression on her face while she thought, "I wish I had friends, but I don't know how to make them."

As the wind swished over to the next house, it stated, "Wow, that looks like fun! Someone is jumping around on a bed! Ah ha ha! Someone is breaking the rules! Ooooooohh ahhhhh. This girl, Nina, has such a messy room full of music notes, dolls, clothes and a bunch of rules written on a lot of paper by her dad. Oh, I doubt she likes to do her chores like cleaning her own room, and washing the dishes, or even feeding the house hamster, even though her dad reminds her about it a billion times each day. Hmm Nina..."

Nina, the musician, was bouncing up and down on her bed to a rhythm, but then lost track of the squeaky beat of the bed springs, and found herself looking through the window.

"I hear music coming from outside to my heart. I'm so happy, and now I will go play my guitar. My dad won't mind it, I think," Nina thought. Nina was just about to pick up her guitar when her dad called her for breakfast.

As the wind flew to the end of the street, it knocked at the window and said, "Sokron Blossom, sleeping in again."

Sokron was such a cute, nice, and tidy color loving girl. She always kept her blonde hair twirled into a ponytail, even at night. Sokron likes to spend all her free time looking through fashion magazines and drawings, and designing girly-girl outfits. She knows that pretty colorful clothes are to die for.

"Sokron! WAKE UP!!" her brother Johnny yelled from the kitchen.

"Wwhhaaatttt?" Sokron yawned in wonder.

Still dreaming, she squealed, "I see pink high heels with a bright pink dress I've always wanted. I'm in h-e-a-v-e-n!"

Sokron lifted her head and bumped into the window, "Oops, that's the window. Good morning reality."

Johnny shouted out to Sokron,

"Get ready Miss Sleepy-Head!"

"Okay," Sokron replied as she got out of her bed, dressed into her fancy blue dress with a cherry on the side, leaving her pajamas on, and rushed to school to meet up with Meeka, Jonsy, and Nina.

Chapter 2

START of SUMMER

Beachwell Elementary School is like a jungle with an extremely large playground full of all kinds of slides, swings, see-saws, bars, and even a rock climbing wall surrounded with yellow and pink poppies.

It was almost the end of the last day of school, a free-uniform day. All students, except Sokron, were ready to hear the final announcement from the school Principal.

"Everyone be quiet. All of us, teachers and staff, are excited about our summer vacation, but you students, have lots and lots of homework that needs to be done during the summer break to prepare for the coming school year," the Princa-apple (as students called him) jokingly laughed over the loud speaker.

"Great! I love homework. And there's 81% of H_2O in the air," Meeka, the science lover, smiled as she looked at her hygrometer watch.

Jonsy, the feeler, felt super boooooored.

Nina mumbled to herself, "Why is he always giving us extra work? I guess he does not like children. Maybe we are too noisy, that's what my dad always says."

"Could you be quiet Nina, you are so loud!" Meeka frowned.

Nina then sighed and said, "Sounds like there are a lot of rules in the world."

"Hey, where's Sokron?" Jonsy wondered.

"Coming!" Sokron shouted as she ran into the classroom.

"I totally forgot about school, I thought it was already summer vacation! Am I late?" Sokron said as she went to her seat and sat down.

"You would have been, if you came one second later," Meeka smiled.

Ding, ding, ding.

"What was that?" Sokron shockingly asked.

Sokron's king-size bed and questioned each other.

"What are we going to do together this summer? I am only here for three days, and then I have to go to math camp. I had a blast last summer: math tests, chess tournaments, calculators, metric system," Meeka happily said.

"What? Huh? Metro what?" they asked as they all looked at her, but Meeka just shrugged her shoulders.

"Well, since I'm so WOW, I'm going to a professional pointy-toes belly dancing camp in three days. I feel so magni-teful!" Jonsy bragged as she posed.

"What does that mean?" Nina wondered.

"I don't know. It just makes me feel good," Jonsy replied.

"I know, Let's have a PINK

SLEEPOVER!" Sokron shouted.

Chapter 3

Pink SLEEPOVER

"SSSleeepooover..." the wind murmured as it flew around the Blossom's house.

Still jumping on Sokron's bed Meeka exclaimed in a fast pace,
"Yeah, we can practice solving math problems all night long!"

"You won't mind me dancing, will ya?" Jonsy asked.

"I would love to stay for a sleepover, but you know my dad with a hundred of his rules," Nina sighed. She stopped jumping and sat down on the bed.

Sokron looked at Nina, sat down next to her, and smiled, "It will be okay."

"Well, it's four o'clock; let's get ready for the sleepover!" Jonsy said as she jumped off the bed with Meeka.

Meeka sat onto Sokron's bed and said, "Let's go to the park first and study blue caterpillars for my science sandwich."

"And I could teach the blue caterpillars to do professional pointy-toed belly dancing," Jonsy giggled. "I'll get them to wear fluffy cherry-pink tutus!" Sokron said with excitement.

"Plus, I can play pop-goes-the-weasel with my guitar, ... trumpet, ... violin, ... banjo, ... and drums. If I had them," Nina said as she daydreamed about those instruments.

"Let's do it," they all shouted. As they happily ran out of Sokron's room and down the street to an enormous park covered with blooming flowers, something caught their eyes: KIKI SHAVER.

Chapter 4

FASHION SHOW

As far as they knew, Kiki Shaver was the meanest girl on the planet.

"Why are you so dressed up?" Sokron asked Kiki as she stared at the puffy purple dress, fish-net leg tights, high black boots, and gold necklaces.

"Because there will be a fashion show at the Shimmering Florida Hotel tomorrow. But of course you're probably not invited to this glamorous, shining event. What a shame!" Kiki sighed with a smile.

47

"Actually, you'll see us there!" Sokron huffed.

Kiki walked away and they all ran back to Sokron's house.

As they entered Sokron's room, Meeka turned and said to the group, "What fashion show?"

"Don't' worry; we still have all night long until the show. And look, Jonsy can do make-up, Nina can do hair styles, you can do accessories, and I can sew pinka-liciously colorful clothes. Oh yeah!" Sokron replied with happiness.

They all looked at Jonsy because she was already upside down dancing on her head and humming America the

Beautiful. Jonsy would always do that when she got very, very, very excited.

"I feel like it's a good idea, but where are we going to get all the supplies? Hum, I know, markers, sharpies, crayons, paint, nail polish, flowers, food coloring, and fruits can be used as make-up for our gorgeous faces, especially mine, mmm," Jonsy smiled.

"We can use macaroni lasagna for hair curls, pasta angel hair for wigs, and peanut butter for gel. I think that should do the trick for hairstyles," Jonsy added.

Still dancing upside down on her head, Jonsy was sweating buckets of water that dripped onto the floor as she thought harder.

She continued to say, "I know! I know! We can use newspapers, plastic bags, leaves, flowers, floppy toys, candy wraps, grass, tape, super glue, dog hair, and stuffed animals to make the clothes! We should start eating lots and lots of candy so that we can have lots of wrappings."

The other three girls froze like icicles as they all stared at Jonsy.

Sokron's dog, Dogon, analyzed the situation and the secret codes, hid under Sokron's yellow couch and whispered, "Agent 55, we are in."

Thirty seconds later, Meeka who was busy thinking about science, asked in confusion, "What about the blue caterpillars? I guess they are not important any more. And why is Jonsy stuffing candy into her mouth? And what is she talking about. Would you please repeat all that, I got lost after the nail polish part." As everyone turned in surprise to Meeka, silence filled the room.

Ignoring Meeka's question, Sokron broke the silence exclaiming "I know! I know! My Babushka has a sewing machine hidden under her bed. I saw it. That means...she must have some fabric somewhere, too."

Chapter 5

BABUSHKA'S ROOM

All the girls tiptoed toward Babushka's room to check on the sewing machine and fabric.

"Don't worry, I know my way," Sokron smiled.

They walked through the small hall full of many identical doors. Sokron put her hand on a door knob, turned to the group, opened the door and said, "We're here!"

53

"I didn't know your grandma lived in the bathroom!" Meeka giggled as she looked at the bathroom sink.

"Just kidding, but does anyone need to go to the bathroom?" Sokron questioned as her cheeks turned beet red.

Sokron closed the bathroom door and went to open the door on her left. Behind that door was a closet. She then opened one other door, opened another door, and another door, and another door, and another door with no success. The girls felt very frustrated and sat on the floor. They began to laugh at each other. Sokron, who rarely went to Babushka's room, tried to open the last door, but she did not have enough strength to pull the door open. She thought to take a little break on the floor, but knew that this was the last chance of finding Babushka's room.

56

Chapter 6

The SEWING MACHINE

Sokron's grandma, Babushka, was a vice-principal at Beachwell Elementary School which was a well kept secret as nobody knew anything about her. She was always prepared for anything possibly thinkable. That's why she always shopped, shopped, shopped. And that's why her room was full of boxes and packages with different spy supplies, all kind of fabrics and clothes, and art craft items.

Chapter 7

The INVITATION

Babushka took out all of the supplies from her wagon and put them on the green, four legged, rectangular table that stood in the middle of Sokron's room.

Grandma quickly left the room to let girls discover themselves and use their talents, and as she closed the door behind her said, "Chop, chop, chop, get to work."

The girls hurried to the table feeling splendid and excited.

"This is my first time for a fashion show," Jonsy screamed into the pink pillow that she grabbed from Sokron's bed.

"Yay! I'm going to look so fantastic in my pink dress and the fabulous bows which will be all over my dress, hair, shoes, gloves, and jewelry. Oh yeah!" Sokron shouted.

"Let's get measuring," Meeka stated as she whipped out a two centimeter long measuring stick from her pocket.

"Oh, I didn't know it was going to be that short," Jonsy replied as she looked at Meeka.

"Lollipop, lollipop, ooo, ooo, ooo, lollipop! Lollipop! Oooo! Ahhhh," Nina sang while she was stared at Babushka's old fashioned sewing machine. She froze with her mouth open as she looked at a sheet of paper hanging from it. She pulled the note off and noticed that it was an invitation from a local newspaper.

It read: "You are invited to be part of a twinkling, sparkling fashion show at Shimmering Florida Hotel on Saturday, June 19th, starting at 8am. Be there to show off your real fashion!"

Nina read the fashion show rules out loud to the rest of the group:

First, must have at least five people on a team.

Second, one model from each team must be at least nine years old.

Third, everyone must have fun!!"

"We can pretend I'm nine, since I am pretty," Jonsy stated as she modeled her poses.

"No. They will probably figure out that you're only seven," Meeka frowned as she measured the fabric on the green table.

The newspaper invitation slipped out of Nina's hand and landed on the floor next to Sokron's bed where Dogon was hiding. He was ready. He jumped out from under the bed, snatched the piece of paper and ran out of the house through the open daisy window.

The four girls noticed that the invitation was gone.

"Dogon took it!" Nina screamed as she pointed to the open window.

The girls zoomed out of the room to chase after the dog. They kept running and running until they bumped right into Dogon. He was sitting on the green grass with a big white bone in his paw smiling at all of them.

Chapter 8

A NEW FRIEND

As the girls were looking at Dogon, Kiki walked toward the group with a happy smile on her face.

"Looking for something?" Kiki asked in a rude way as she waved the invitation in her hand.

"You only have four people on your team. Bummer. Looks like you all are definitely NOT going to win. Better luck next year!" she stated.

"Well, there is a way we can both win. Would you want to join our group for the show?" suggested Sorkon in a shaky voice.

"And you're nine, so that'll be perfect," added Jonsy.

"And we both need five people in a group," smiled Meeka awkwardly.

The four girls looked at each other scared, but knew it was the only way to go.

Kiki battled with her brain, "Yes, or no? Huuuummm. Yes? Maybe. NO! Why not, I don't get along with others, so maybe I should not. Yes. I guess it could be fun. No, I'm afraid to show who I really am. Yes, I want to win first place. Maybe not, I am afraid to share my feelings. Yes, I guess I should try to turn my life around.   YES, most definitely."

"YES," Kiki whispered.

"Ah ha, oh yeah, we're going to the fashion show," Nina cheered.

"Let's do it!" Sokron shouted.

"Oh my gosh! We only have 13 ¼ hours left before the show starts!" Meeka shouted.

The four excited girls flipped, cart-wheeled, skipped, and jumped over to 'Home-Sweet-Home' Sokron's rosy room once again.

"You guys! Wait for me," Kiki shouted as she hurried after the crazy fun girls.

Dogon whispered, "Agent 55, a new friendship is getting stitched." up."

69

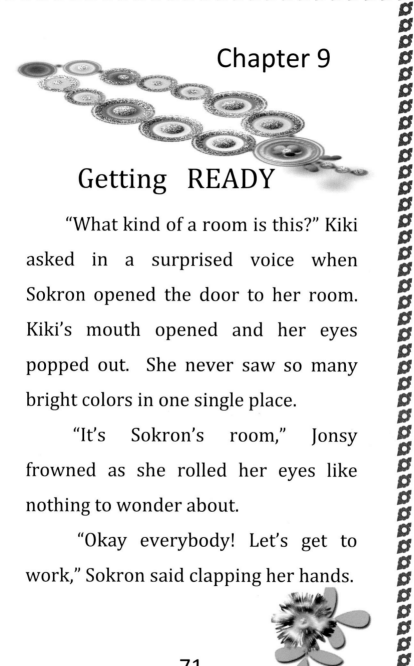

Chapter 9

Getting READY

"What kind of a room is this?" Kiki asked in a surprised voice when Sokron opened the door to her room. Kiki's mouth opened and her eyes popped out. She never saw so many bright colors in one single place.

"It's Sokron's room," Jonsy frowned as she rolled her eyes like nothing to wonder about.

"Okay everybody! Let's get to work," Sokron said clapping her hands.

71

All the girls started to do their thing when Kiki asked, "What am I supposed to do? Look pretty or what?"

"Well, you can watch TV downstairs, play a fashion video game, or help us out," Nina stated.

"Yeah, you can help with the hairstyles, the make-up, the sewing, or the accessories," Sokron said.

"I got it," Kiki answered as she ran between the girls to tell them how she wanted to look for the fashion show. Kiki discovered and never knew that helping others can actually help her as well.

Time passed with much screaming, yelling, laughing, tripping, dancing, falling, singing, sewing, and snoring as the girls got closer to getting ready for the show with their newly made designer clothes and matching accessories.

"Wake up Sokron! It's time to go now," they all shouted as they shook her awake. Sokron opened her sleepy eyes still dreaming and pointed to Kiki and said, "Who is that? She is so pretty and I just love her taste." Then Sokron remembered they were all preparing for the fashion show.

"Thanks," Kiki replied.

"Let's go!" they all yelled.

Chapter 10

The Adventure

"Wait! Girls!" Sokron yawned as she rubbed her eyes. "How are we even going to get there? I don't even know where it's at."

Meeka was calculating the exact distance from Sokron's green table to the Shimmering Florida Hotel's backstage including the three steps at Hotel's front door.

"It's only twenty-five miles to the show! We can totally make it there in 2 ½ days if we walked at a speed of 3 miles per hour, took two-hour naps, had bathroom breaks, and ate yummy snacks," Meeka shared with the girls.

During all that time while the girls were busy having fun with designing, measuring, sewing, crafting, face painting (make-up), and running around with preparation for the fashion show, Sokron's grandma, Babushka, was in her room relaxing on her high soft bed as she stared at the newest big screen on her wall. She smiled.

"Wow! What is she watching?" the wind wondered as it sneaked through her window.

"A movie or something? Oh, NO, I don't believe it. It is Sokron's room.

That is what she is sneaking about," the wind whispered to itself in surprise.

When the girls were almost ready to leave the house and bombard each other with questions about how to get to the show in time, Babushka knew that it was time for her to show up.

She tiptoed toward Sokron's room, hiding behind the door and quietly counted, "one, two, three".

"Are you ladies ready for this fashion show?" Grandma shouted as she barged into the room.

"Um, o-k-a-y, I guess we're ready as we'll ever be," Nina replied as she looked at the other girls.

They all followed Sokron's grandma over to her old fashioned multi-seated motor bike.

"Hop on and hold tight! We'll be there in no time," grandma said enthusiastically.

The girls all jumped into the vehicle with excitement and nervousness. They shut their eyes tight ready to take off in a flash.

"La la la, hop on and hold tight, don't forget your light. We'll be there in no time, don't forget to bring a dime," Nina sang cheerfully.

"Hey, umm, we're not zooming along as fast as we all expected," complained Nina.

Grandma reminded them it was her old fashioned long-as-a-boat motor bike and NOT a high-speed-racing-vehicle.

At 7:59am they arrived at the Shimmering Florida Hotel.

"We have five seconds left before the show starts. And can somebody please wake up Sokron again?" said Meeka. Since Sokron loves to sleep so much, using her imagination made her full of exhaustion.

"Hey look, there's a colorful pink dress!" Nina shouted.

"What!? Where?" Sokron asked as she jumped up from her sleep.

The other girls giggled.

Meeka ran excitedly over to the backstage area as she followed the signs pointing to the stage.

"Hold on Meeka, you're running too fast! And how do you run in high heels?" Kiki yelled.

The girls chased after Meeka, while the grandma locked up her motor bike.

As they got near the fashion show backstage area, the security guard answered, "Are you ladies in the fashion show?"

"Yes, we are!" Sokron smiled as she tried to catch her breath.

"What's the name of your team and model?" the guard frowned.

"Umm, our team name is, is, um, 'Friendship.' And the model's name is Kiki Shaver and she is definitely nine years old. And here are the names of the designers," replied Sokron as she handed a piece of paper to the guard.

As the girls got Kiki totally ready in the backstage area, the host in the brown suit with small colored hearts announced into the microphone, "Ladies and gentlemen, last but not least, is ... KIKI SHAVER, from the 'FRIENDSHIP' team."

The girls then walked over to the middle of the glamorously decorated stage tightly holding their hands and smiling as wide as they possibly could. They were happy and nervous, cheerful and jittery.

Kiki stood in front of her team and as she posed and walked on the runway, the announcer continued,

"The designers of the team include: Sokron, who created this wonderfully fantastically outstanding dress using rainbow colors. Meeka, who made the beautifully astonishing jewelry; just look at those sparkling earrings and the pinkish blue pearl necklace worn by Kiki. And guess who did her hair? It's an extraordinary hair style done by Nina. And last of the 'Friendship' team is Jonsy. What kind of make-up did you use? It's gorgeous and brilliant.

And again, let me introduce their model, Kiki Shaver!"

When Kiki finished the runway and took her bow, the people cheered louder than ever. The girls all felt happy and excited.

As the green curtains were lowered to close the show, Kiki's heart sang joyfully as she went to hug the girls.

"It's so fun having friends," Kiki said as she squeezed her new BFF's.

"Well, Kiki, it's good to have you on the team," said Jonsy.

"Let's go home now, I'm way exhausted!" Sokron yawned.

They all laughed and headed toward the motorcycle holding hands.

Kiki thanked the girls for letting her be their friend.

"Isn't it fun sewing friendships?" Sokron asked.

"It sure is!" they all replied.

When they arrived at Sokron's house, her dad asked, "Oh! Hey girls, what trouble were you up to the first day of summer break?"

"Just a few little girly things. Nothing too exciting," Sokron replied with a smile as the other girls laughed.

.

"Agent 55, the case is clear," Dogon, Sokron's dog, reported from the rose bushes under her window.

"Awesome job! Let's go PARTY!!!" Babushka whispered into the dog's ear.

The End

To the best Pink Sleepover ever.